W9-BAL-205

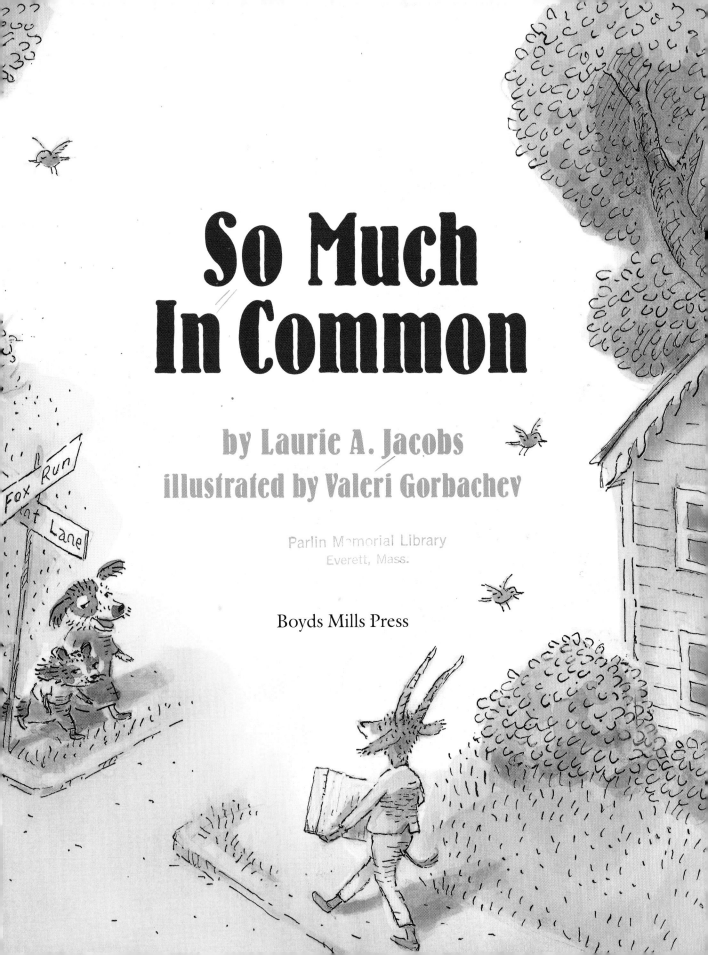

So Much In Common

by Laurie A. Jacobs
illustrated by Valeri Gorbachev

Parlin Memorial Library
Everett, Mass.

Boyds Mills Press

For my parents, Estelle and Julius, who set me on the right path,
and for Steven, who walks it with me
L.A.J.

To my wife, Victoria, and to my children, Sasha and Konstantin
V.G.

Text copyright © 1994 by Laurie A. Jacobs
Illustrations copyright © 1994 by Boyds Mills Press
All rights reserved

Published by Caroline House
Boyds Mills Press, Inc.
A Highlights Company
815 Church Street
Honesdale, Pennsylvania 18431
Printed in Mexico

Publisher Cataloging-in-Publication Data
Jacobs, Laurie A.
      So much in common / by Laurie A. Jacobs ; illustrated by
Valeri Gorbachev.—1st ed.
[32]p. : col. ill. ; cm.
Summary : A tale of two good friends who can accept each
other's differences.
ISBN 1-56397-115-1
[1. Friendship—Fiction.] I. Gorbachev, Valeri, ill. II. Title.
[E]—dc20   1994
Library of Congress Catalog Card Number 92-73995

First edition, 1994
Book designed by Leslie Bauman
The text of this book is set in 14-point Galliard Roman.
The illustrations are done in pen and ink and watercolors.
Distributed by St. Martin's Press

10 9 8 7 6 5 4 3 2 1

Philomena Midge lived in an old house on Pheasant Lane.

Horace Abercrombie lived in a new house on Fox Run.

Their friends said they had nothing in common but their backyard fence.

Philomena liked to collect things. Her house was filled with stuff. "It does seem a bit crowded," she admitted, "but you never know when something will come in handy."

Horace preferred the spare, uncluttered look. "If it's not essential, out it goes," he told his friends.

Philomena liked to cook. She was always experimenting with new dishes. "Mmmm," she said, licking a spoon. "Cooking is such fun."

Horace ate only take-out food. "Cooking is a bore," he said.

Philomena liked to garden. Her backyard overflowed with flowers. "I just can't get enough of a good thing," she said to Horace.

Horace liked to garden, too. He had a Japanese-style garden with lots of rocks and tiny bushes. "It's very peaceful," he explained to Philomena.

One day Philomena invited Horace to dinner. "After all," she said to him, "what good is cooking if you have no one to share it with?"

Horace ate everything Philomena served and asked for seconds. "Philomena," he said, patting his stomach, "that was the best meal I've ever eaten."

The next day, Horace called to Philomena over the fence. "Would you like to hear a joke?" he asked.

"Oh, yes," said Philomena. "I love a good joke."

"What happened to the farmer's eggs when she washed them?" Horace asked.

"I don't know," said Philomena. "What?"

"Nothing," said Horace. "But you should have seen those eggs when she tried to wring them dry!"

Philomena chuckled. "That's a good one, Horace. Tell me some more!"

From then on, Philomena and Horace spent almost every day together. Their friends didn't understand.

"Whatever do you see in that Philomena?" Horace's friends asked him.

"I don't know," said Horace. "But she likes my jokes, and she cooks like a dream."

"Whatever do you see in that Horace?" Philomena's friends asked her.

"I don't know," said Philomena. "But he loves what I cook, and he tells the funniest jokes."

One day Philomena was riding her bicycle through town when she spotted an old umbrella that someone had thrown away. She opened it up.

"This would be perfect for Horace," she said.

Philomena pedaled off as fast as she could. She was so busy admiring the umbrella that she didn't see Horace coming out of the pizza parlor carrying an extra-large anchovy pizza. Philomena rode straight into him. There was pizza everywhere.

"I'm so sorry," said Philomena as she tried to help Horace clean up. "But I found this umbrella for you and . . . " Philomena noticed an anchovy hanging from Horace's ear, and she burst out laughing.

Horace was furious.

"You ruined my dinner and my good suit for an old umbrella, and then you have the nerve to laugh at me!" Horace shouted.

"Oh, Horace," Philomena said. "Don't be so serious, it really is quite funny!" And she laughed some more.

"You can keep your crummy umbrella!" Horace fumed. "I'm going home."

How rude! thought Philomena.

How inconsiderate! thought Horace.

"That's just like Philomena," Horace's friends said to him.
"You should ignore her from now on."

"What else could you expect from that Horace?" Philomena's friends said to her. "You should never speak to him again."

After that, Philomena and Horace didn't talk to each other. They didn't even wave over their backyard fence.

Philomena soon lost interest in cooking. Horace stopped telling jokes. They missed each other.

Days went by. Philomena saw an announcement that the garden club was holding a competition for the best flower arrangement.

"Well, why not enter," she said to herself, "now that I have all this time on my hands." Philomena gathered a huge armload of flowers from her garden and put them in a big silver bucket.

Horace read the same announcement.

"I might as well enter," he sighed. "It will give me something to do." He took a black bowl, filled it with water, and floated three perfect rose petals in it.

All Philomena's friends thought she should win. "That Horace is just too odd," they told Philomena. Philomena said nothing.

All Horace's friends thought he should win. "That Philomena overdoes everything," they told Horace. Horace didn't reply.

Horace and Philomena tied for first place.

"You know," Horace said to Philomena,
"I was rooting for you. Your flowers reminded me
of a meadow on a sunny summer day."

"That's funny," said Philomena. "I hoped you'd win.
Your arrangement made me think of a cool summer rain."

They both laughed.

"I'm sorry I was so rude to you,"
said Horace.

"I'm sorry I was so inconsiderate,"
said Philomena.

They went out for ice cream. Philomena ordered the passion fruit surprise. Horace ordered a scoop of plain vanilla. They sat close together and held hands.

"Horace," Philomena whispered, "I have some new recipes to try for you."

"Philomena," Horace whispered back, "I have some new jokes to tell you."

"But, Philomena!" said her friends.

"But, Horace!" said his friends.

"It will never work!"

"Don't be silly," said Horace and Philomena together. "After all, we have so much in common!"